Peppa Pig

Hide-and-Seek

A Search and Find Book

Fun and Games

Peppa and her friends are playing hide-and-seek.
Peppa is very good at hiding.

"I want to hide now!" says Suzy Sheep.
"Me, too," says Danny Dog, "but it's time
to go!"
"Let's play this afternoon," says Peppa.
"You can hide and I will seek!"

But everyone has to go out this afternoon.

Can you spot: 5 drawings 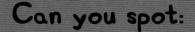   1 jack-in-the-box

1 horn

2 cars

the Sun

In the Garden

Peppa tells Daddy Pig that her friends are not all going to be in the same place for hide-and-seek. "Why don't I help you find your friends, Peppa?" says Daddy Pig.

"What a good idea!" says Mummy Pig. "You can start by finding George. He's hiding in the garden."

Can you help Peppa and Daddy Pig find George?

Coming, ready or not!

Can you spot:

George

1 bird feeder

2 bees

3 butterflies   **4** orange roses   **5** red apples

At the Playground

Daddy Pig takes Peppa and George to the playground. It is very busy. George has fun playing in the sandpit while Peppa looks for Emily Elephant.

Can you spot:

 Emily Elephant

Mr Dinosaur

2 green buckets

Tweet! Tweet!

Wheeeee!

3 kites   4 red spades  the number 5

At the Gym

Next, Daddy Pig takes Peppa and George to the gym to find Suzy Sheep.
"Are you going to join us, Daddy Pig?" asks Mummy Sheep.
"Oh no," says Daddy Pig, "I have to look after Peppa and George."

Baa!

Can you spot:

Suzy Sheep

1 shiny silver whistle

2 golf clubs

3 rugby balls

4 black and white footballs

5 exercise bikes

In the Library

At the library, Daddy Pig returns a book.
"You've had this book out for ten years!"
says Miss Rabbit.
"Sorry," says Daddy Pig, "*The Wonderful World of Concrete* is very interesting!"

Sssh!

Can you spot:

Zoe Zebra

Daddy Pig's book

A computer

2 books about tigers

3 paintings in golden frames

4 chairs

At the Museum

Next, Peppa looks for Pedro Pony in George's favourite
room at the museum — the dinosaur room!
Daddy Pig's favourite room is the museum café.
"Maybe we can go there next," says Daddy Pig. "Ho! Ho!"

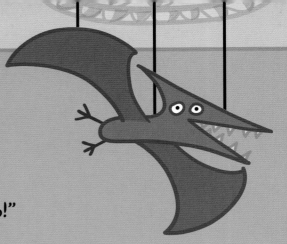

Grrr! Grrr!

Can you spot:

Pedro Pony

1 shiny crown

2 exploding volcanoes

3 golden goblets

4 dinosaur eggs

A dinosaur skeleton

On the River

Ahoy there! On the way to the boatyard, Peppa sees Grandpa Pig's boat. Grandad Dog is towing it to the boatyard for repairs.

Squawk! Pretty Polly!

Can you spot:

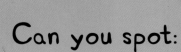

Danny Dog

1 bell

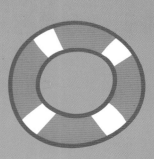

2 red and white lifebelts

3 life
jackets

4 coils
of rope

5 yellow ducks

At the Supermarket

At the supermarket, Peppa looks for Rebecca Rabbit while Daddy Pig finds the things on his shopping list.
"Was that chocolate cake on the list, Daddy?" asks Peppa.
"Let's pretend it was," says Daddy Pig.
"It looks so delicious!"

Crunch! Crunch!

Can you spot:

 Rebecca Rabbit

 1 very large melon

 2 green shopping bags

Hee! Hee!

Snort!

3 baguettes

4 jars of marmalade

5 jars of honey

At the Fire Station

It's time to pick up Mummy Pig from the fire station. All the mummies have been at Firefighter Practice.
"Oh look!" says Daddy Pig. "There's a nice cup of tea and some biscuits."

Can you spot:

Candy Cat

1 fire engine alarm

2 hoses for squirting water

3 fire extinguishers

4 wheels

5 firefighter helmets

Muddy Puddles

Everyone goes back to Peppa's house for tea.
"Should we play hide-and-seek again, Peppa?"
asks Danny Dog. "It's your turn to hide."
"We have used all the hiding places!" says Peppa.
"Let's jump in muddy puddles!"

Everyone loves jumping in muddy puddles!

Hee
Hee

Hee
Hee

Squelch!

Splish!

Can you spot:

1 wolf

2 rabbits

Splash!

Squelch!

Squelch!

3 zebras

4 pairs of red wellies

5 cookies

Where's Peppa?

Peppa visited all of these places in her game of hide-and-seek. Can you see her hiding somewhere in this picture?